PRI   Park, Margaret
PAR   Now For My Next Number!
              Songs for Multiplying Fun

Now for My Next Number!

Songs for Multiplying Fun

Margaret Park

Pictures by Sophia Esterman

Great River Books

Salt Lake City

For information contact:
    Great River Books
    161 M Street
    Salt Lake City, Utah 84103

    www.greatriverbooks.com

Library of Congress Cataloging-in-Publication Data

Park, Margaret, 1954-
  Now for my next number! : songs for multiplying fun / Margaret Park ; pictures by Sophia Esterman.
    p. cm.
  ISBN 978-0-915556-38-0 (hardcover)
  1. Multiplication--Juvenile literature. 2. Counting--Juvenile literature. 3. Music in mathematics education--Juvenile literature. I. Esterman, Sophia, 1979-, ill. II. Title.
  QA115.P256 2007
  513.2'13--dc22
                          2007008185
                          103748

Manufactured in Mexico

Shoes in Twos
Counting by 2

Do you see those shoes?
Do you hear their beat?
Two by two
Walking down the street
2, 4, 6, 8, 10 and 12

They don't talk
They just walk
Hot off the shelves
Keeping to themselves

They don't talk
They just walk

14, 16, 18 and more
20, 22, 24

Hot off the shelves
Keeping to themselves
They don't talk
They just walk

Thirty-six Witches on a Halloween Day

Counting by 3

Thirty-six witches
Packed their lunch and dishes
And set out for a trip
To the briny seashore
Flying to their picnic
Three on a broomstick
For sandwiches by
The sparkling sea

Then 3, 6, 9
Went surfing on the brine

12, 15, 18
Racing brooms this Halloween

21, 24, 27
Loopity-looping
the heavens

30, 33, 36
Contemplating dirty-tricks

36 witches on a
Halloween Day

Doing the Happy Dance
Counting by 4

Red sun beaming on a big meadow
Nighthawks streaming through a bright rainbow
The evening air was falling soft and sweet
Drumming with the sound of animal feet

At the happy dance
At the happy dance
They're doing the happy dance
Down at the Happy dance

4 camel knobby knees a-knocking
8 turtle legs tilting and a-rocking
12 donkey legs kick up their hooves
16 cat paws doing soft-shoe moves

At the happy dance
Down at the happy dance
They're doing the happy dance
Down at the happy dance

20 gator legs slow and plodding
24 foxy feet fast fox-trotting
28 rabbit feet go hippity hop
32 horse shoes go clippity clop

At the happy dance
At the happy dance

They're doing the happy dance
Down at the happy dance

36 giraffe sticks in a Tango dance
40 lambskin boots do a Go-Go prance
44 leopard paws in a spotty Twist
48 mice feet in the rising mist

At the happy dance
Doing the happy dance
They love the happy dance
Let's do the happy dance

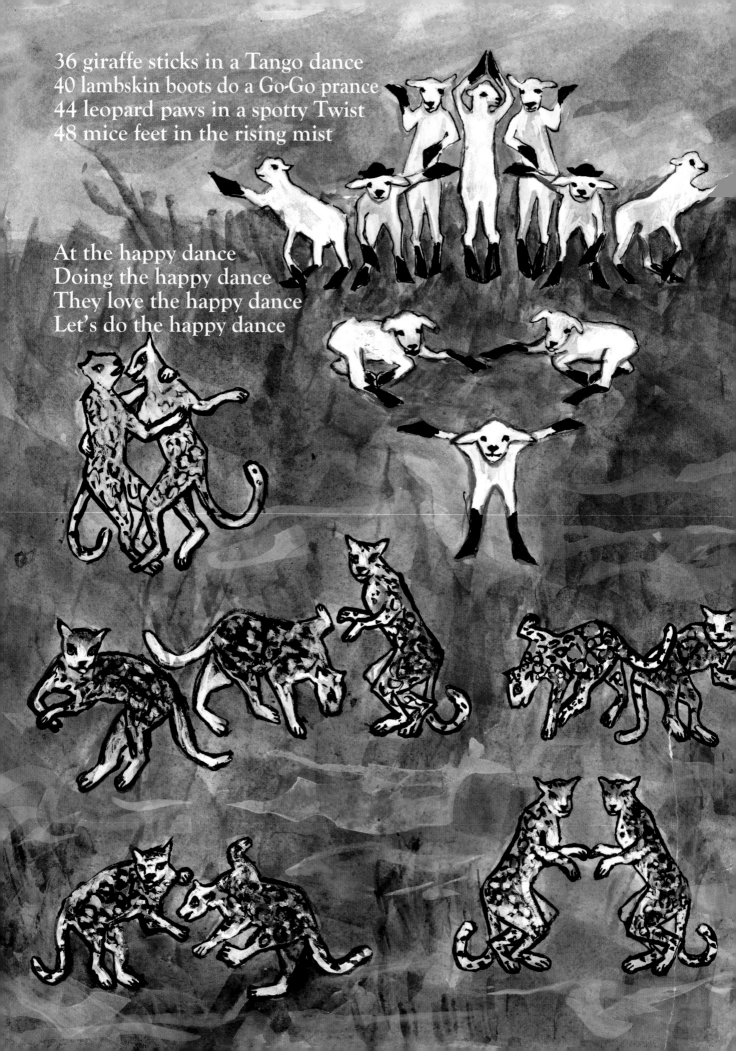

A Whole Lot of Hippos
Counting by 5

A whole lot of hippos heaped in a huddle
Wallowed together in a deep mud puddle

5, then 10, then 15
Swam in the river and came out clean

20, 25, 30
We're happy staying dirty

50, 55, 60
Played in the shade of the baobab tree

Rhyme Crime Rap
Counting by 6

In a land I once saw
They had a very funny law
That every rhyme was a crime
And you might have to pay a fine
They could grab you by the collar
Make you pay six dollars
For your rhyme crime
Every single time

Once - 6 bucks
Twice - 12 bucks
Thrice - 18 bucks
Four times is 24 dollars

f you said green bean
And that you grew too few
Then the law of that land
Could write a ticket to you

Say you play honky-tonky
On the hurdy-gurdy
Get poetic and wordy
You'd end up paying thirty

Five times is 30 bucks
Six times is 36 bucks
Seven times is 42 dollars
Eight times is 48 dollars

So, if you visit that land
You'd better stick to this plan
Put your hand on your pocket
Zip your mouth up and lock it
To keep from going wrong
Never ever sing this song

Nine is 54 bucks
Ten is 60 bucks
Eleven - 66 bucks
Twelve is 72 dollars

Sinbad Sailed the Seven Seas
Counting by 7

Oh, Sinbad sailed the Seven Seas
In a golden galleon on a gentle breeze
He left early one morning without saying a word
With his telescope and his secretary bird
Listen if you want to know what Sinbad saw
As he sailed the seas from shore to shore

He saw
7 frogmen
14 mermaids preen
21 flying fish run
28 penguins skate

He saw
35 submarines dive
42 whales turn blue

49 pelicans dine
56 dragon chicks

He saw
63 sailors see
70 pirates flee

77 motors revin'
84 oysters snore

Oh, Sinbad sailed from
Shore to shore
From shore to shore
Until there wasn't any more

At Eight
Counting by 8

At the stroke of eight in the dark of night
I walk the road in the pale moonlight
My vision so hazy, my hearing so clear
The dark night world comes in through my ear
8 church bell rings, 16 rushing wings
24 loon calls, 32 footfalls

And the stars appear by a mighty force
East to west in the nightly course

My eyes adjusted to the soft dim light
See the magic glow of the world tonight

40 paper moons
48 raccoons

56 aspen eyes
64 fireflies

72 swans, 80 stars in the ponds
88 goose bumps, 96 heart jumps
And the stars appear by a mighty force
East to west in the nightly course
And I feel the pulling of a million stars
So near they are, right here they are

And the stars appear by a mighty force
East to west in the nightly course

Nine Lives
Counting by 9

They say every cat has nine whole lives
They act a little risky and a little unwise
Scratching his back on the windowsill
A cat falls off, takes a two-story spill

9, 18, 27
Kitty cats landing at the gates of heaven

Pausing on their way to the heavenly door

We're not dead; let's have a little more fun

90, 99, 108
Leaping back to life
from the pearly gates

Twelve Islands in the Sun
Counting by 12

Twelve islands shining in the sun
Under the water they all were one
Sunny shores kissed by the wavy sea
Each island had a big banana tree

There were
12 big banana trees
24 little monkeys
36 purple parakeets
48 flowers smell so sweet

There were
60 black and gold bumble bees
72 jumping monkey fleas
84 shiny beetles munching, on
96 bananas bunching

There were
108 banana thieves
120 banana leaves
132 peels on the ground
144 slugs all around

Twelve islands shining in the sun
Under the water they all were one
Sunny shores kissed by the wavy sea
Each island had a big banana tree

This book and music CD can be enjoyed by children of many ages. Preschoolers can enjoy the lively stories and pictures in the book and learn each number and its multiples as words to songs. The vivid lyrics, the use of rhythm, rhyme, melodies and pictures will help children memorize number patterns to provide a good foundation for later learning to multiply. When a child is ready to learn multiplication, the illustrations can clarify math concepts by showing countable objects that represent the number, how many times it is multiplied and the resulting product.

Children can use these songs to memorize the times tables if they keep track of the multiple by extending a finger (or fingers and toes) while they sing the product number (as illustrated below). This book doesn't include songs for counting by 10 or by 11. These sequences are very clear and easy to memorize without the aid of songs. Children can be taught to count by ten and by eleven and then can practice the ten and eleven times tables by extending fingers as below.

Example from Shoes in Twos

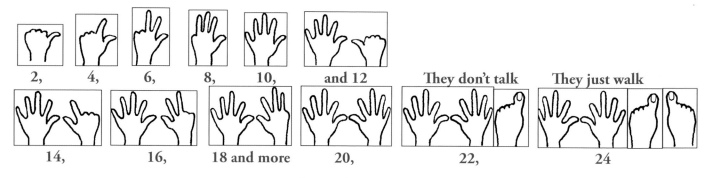

About the Artists

Margaret Park is a children's book author and an editor of books on child development, brain-based learning, and innovative teaching methods. She wrote the lyrics for all of the songs, and composed the melodies and sang the vocal parts for *Thirty-Six Witches, Sinbad Sailed the Seven Seas, At Eight*, and *Nine Lives*. This is her fourth children's book.

Sophia Esterman is a painter, print maker, and illustrator. She drew and painted all the pictures in the book, including those 108 cats and 108 hutias (the banana thieves in the twelve song). She lives in New York City with Mike, a jazz performer, and their cat Naima. www.sophiaesterman.com

Troy Lennerd Nielsen is a performer and composer whose musical compositions have been performed in the United States, Europe and China. He has been a recipient of the Margaret Jory Fairbanks Copyright Assistant Grant and his compositions have received awards and honors from the American Music Center, ASCAP, and The Composer's Guild. Troy Lennerd Nielsen composed, arranged, and played all the parts except vocals for *A Whole Lot of Hippos, Rhyme Crime Rap* and *Twelve Islands in the Sun*. Troy lives in Salt Lake City with his wife Eva and dogs, Joshu and Willow. www.troylennerd.com

Bruce Lambson started on drums and later switched to guitar and bass in high school. He toured for years throughout Seattle and the Pacific Northwest with the hard rock band *Road Apple Roy and the Steaming Noogies*. He was also a booking agent and band manager for Farwest Entertainment. Currently he writes, composes and records solo music projects under the name Mo Bruder. Bruce composed the music and played all the parts including vocals for, *Shoes in Twos, and The Happy Dance*. He's also the vocalist for *A Whole Lot of Hippos, Rhyme Crime Rap* and *Twelve Islands in the Sun*. He lives in Salt Lake City with his wife Annie and their cat Radar.

Ahti Mohala did the musical arrangements and played all the parts except guitar and vocals on the songs; *Thirty-Six Witches, Sinbad Sailed the Seven Seas, At Eight*, and *Nine Lives*. In addition to arranging and composing he's a popular and versatile multi-instrumentalist whose performing and recording credits keep him active in many venues. He lives on the "big island" of Hawaii with his wife Jamilla and cat Stanley who can be heard making his meowsic debut in the song *Nine Lives*. Ahti Mohala c/o Worldwin Ent. P.O. Box 338 Captain Cook Hawaii 96704

Engineering, Mixing, and Guitar for the background music of *Thirty-six Witches, Sinbad Sailed the Seven Seas, At Eight*, and *Nine Lives* by L.T. "Smooth" @ JenZan Productions Leon_Jenny90@hotmail.com